# Sitka Tango

## Lost in the Park

Writing, Photos and Illustrations by
**Tracie and Grace Harang**

Copyright © 2012 by Tracie and Grace Harang

Soft Cover ISBN: 978-1-57833-598-5
Hard Cover ISBN: 978-1-57833-953-2
Edited by: Sandra Fontaine (Grace's Grandma)
Design: Vered R. Mares, Todd Communications

Published by:
**Sitka Tango Publishing**

122 Anna Drive
Sitka, AK 99835

907-738-5040 • www.sitkatango.com
Distributed by Todd Communications
611 E. 12th Ave., Suite 102
Anchorage, AK 99501-4603
(907) 274-TODD (8633) • Fax (907) 929-5550
sales@toddcom.com • WWW.ALASKABOOKSANDCALENDARS.COM
with other offices in Ketchikan, Juneau and Fairbanks, Alaska.

Printed by Everbest Printing Co., Ltd., in Guangzhou, China,
through **Alaska Print Brokers**, Anchorage, Alaska.

*Exploring Totem Poles in Sitka National Historical Park*

# Dedication

For my three wonderful children
I love you more than the stars love the moon.
Love, Mom

For Tango
Thank you for being such a fun dog!
You are the highlight of my life.
Love, Grace

# Acknowledgments

Thank you to the caretakers of Sitka National Historical Park. Sitka is fortunate to have such a beautiful park to visit. A special thank you to Tom Gamble for being our guide, and Becky Latanich for your help reviewing our book.

Thank you to Tommy Joseph for your dedication to carving and your time to look over our project.

Tracie Harang
Explore!

Tango is a Nova Scotia Duck Tolling Retriever. He has been a wonderful dog and is naturally photogenic! Please note that we did have special permission from the Park Service to allow Tango to be off leash in the park during our photo shoots. Normally dogs are not allowed off leash in the park. We hope that you enjoy reading about Tango, Grace and their adventure in Sitka National Historical Park!

This is our third book in our Sitka Tango series. You can order more copies of our books on our website.

**www.sitkatango.com**

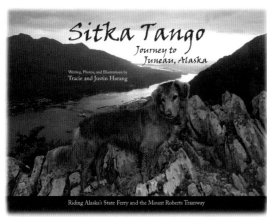

Woof! I am a dog named Tango. I love to play and explore with my family who lives in Sitka, Alaska. I love kids! I have three kids to play with, but with the "brothers" getting older, Grace gives me the most attention. Grace takes me on kayak rides in the ocean, walks on trails, throws the ball for me and snuggles with me. I love Grace for all of these reasons. She is my buddy and we have had many adventures together.

One such adventure happened just last year...

One day, despite the rain and wind, Grace's first grade class was taking
a field trip to Sitka National Historical Park. I got some awesome news!
I was invited on the field trip with my best friend Grace!
This was certainly "dog bone" (super) exciting!

Tango thought.

Sandwiched between the beautiful, majestic
mountains of Baranof Island and the chilly Pacific
Ocean in Southeast Alaska, lies Alaska's smallest
national park, Sitka National Historical Park.

The park is the home of many special totem poles. The totem poles have been carved by Tlingit and Haida Natives. These totem poles are cut down, carved trees that tell stories. The talented carvers use animals and some humans to tell a special story from the bottom to the top of the pole.

*Grace's class had a very nice park employee named Ranger Tom Gamble to explain the totem poles and lead the class through the park. Grace's class listened carefully to Ranger Tom as he described the totem poles. I was quietly patient, but could not wait to get into the woods, where the squirrels play!*

Tango said to himself.

As we wandered into the park, the huge canopy of spruce and hemlock trees protected us from the wind and the rain. The class stopped and talked about the tall totem poles. On one totem pole, Ranger Tom pointed out the Native watchman atop the pole whose colorful hat rings told of his wealth.

Very interesting, but the squirrel chirping to my right was even more exciting to me!

Tango thought.

Grace had the job of carrying the class camera and taking photos of interesting things in the forest. As Grace was taking a picture of a common local tree fungus called bear bread, I saw a squirrel run right in front of me! In my squirrel frenzy, I forgot that I was attached to Grace by a leash! I pulled so fast and hard that it pulled her over and made her drop her camera.

Tango said.

Grace was mad at me and scolded me for pulling. Once she stood up and brushed herself off, Grace yelled, "Oh no, now we are way behind!" Quickly, off we ran to catch up, forgetting all about the camera laying on the forest floor.

Tango thought.

13

*It did not take us long to catch up with the class. We listened to Ranger Tom as he told us some of the interesting facts about each carving on the totem pole. Just as Grace was reaching into her pocket for her camera, my keen dog ears heard her mumble, "Oh no, my camera!" Grace looked very worried and handed my leash to a friend.*

Tango thought.

*All of a sudden, Grace sneaked into some brush nearby and disappeared! No one noticed but me, I always notice what Grace is doing.*

15

As for Grace, she was busy thinking about the camera. She must have left it by the bear bread! Grace made a decision. She did not want to get into trouble for being careless with the camera. So, she had decided to sneak back alone and not tell anyone where she was going. (Later, Grace would realize that this was not a good decision.)

Grace took a back trail so that the class would not see her. She jumped over branches and ran down the trail as fast as she could go. She wanted to get the camera and return to her class before they realized she was missing!

*I did not like being separated from Grace, but I was on a leash, so what could I do? We soon reached a large open field with a beautiful totem pole standing tall and mighty right in the middle of the field. Grace's teacher turned to ask Grace to take a picture, but Grace was nowhere to be found! The students looked at one another hoping to see Grace, but she was missing! That is when they all turned to me, the dog who was being ignored. Grace's teacher asked me to find Grace!*

They led me to the last totem pole where they remembered Grace standing and then let me go! I knew exactly what to do. I play hide and seek with Grace all the time, and she always gives me a yummy treat once I find her!

I ran like lightning down the trail, with her scent in my nose! This field trip just became so much more exciting!

In the meantime Grace had found her camera and was trying to find the class. She ran back to the field where she thought the class would be, but it was not there. She was suddenly very worried. Why had she not passed her class on the trail? Which way should she go to look for her class?

While wandering alone in the park, Grace began speaking to the totem poles. First, she thought to speak to the watchman. Grace said, "Hey you, sitting so high in the sky, please tell me, Mr. Watchman, do you spy my class?" He said nothing, not a sound.

Grace wandered on until she spotted a momma beaver holding her baby. "Please Mrs. Beaver, the way you snuggle your baby beaver makes me miss my mom too. With your keen ears, have you heard my class calling for me?" Mrs. Beaver said nothing, not a sound.

Grace continued down the trail where she had last seen her class and noticed Mr. Hawk gazing out over Sitka Sound. "Ok Mr. Hawk, I have always heard that hawks are smart. If you were looking for your class in this park, which direction would you go?" He said nothing, not a sound.

Grace backtracked a bit more and found another totem pole that she had passed by. She had passed it because of the shrimp. The shrimp figure on a totem pole often represents a cheater and a liar. The last thing Grace was in the mood for was a lie. However, with a big sigh and a dreadful feeling of being lost, she took her chances with Mr. Shrimp. "OK Mr. Shrimp, I have been back and forth on this trail looking for my class, I am worried. I am lost and I need help. Please, no lies today. I am not in the mood. I have spoken to the tall watchman, the protective beaver, the wise hawk and now you. Can you please look me in the eye and tell me what to do?" He said nothing, not a sound.

Grace lowered her head, then wandered down the trail to a bench by the ocean where she sat with a feeling of dread in her stomach. Grace knew that her teacher must be so worried! She knew she would be in big trouble.

*Back on the trail, I was hot on Grace's scent. I was close, very, very close...*

Tango thought.

*Shortly, after much tracking back and forth in the park, I burst out of the woods and found Grace sitting on a bench. I could not stop licking her, I was so relieved! I then lifted my chin and started to howl like a wolf! Grace had never seen me do this before, but I knew that it would lead the search party to us!*

*Grace hugged me and hugged me! I thought she would never let go!*

Soon, Grace's entire class was surrounding us. Everyone was very glad to see us. They seemed glad that we were both okay. However, we had to get back to school.

The class then made Grace and me walk with a friend in front of the teacher all the way back to Baranof School. Everyone was wet and cold, but happy that we were all together!

*When Grace got to class, her teacher asked her for the camera*
*and asked Grace if she took any pictures during her journey.*
"Well," Grace replied, "yes, just one..."

The end

Grace Harang

Left: Raven Memorial Pole

Right: "Trees on fire" sunset and totem pole in the park.

Left: Sitka, Alaska welcomes visitors from all over the world. During the summer many visitors arrive on cruise ships such as this one. These ships anchor just off shore of downtown Sitka and Sitka National Historical Park. This photograph shows the vessel "Oosterdam" sandwiched between Sitka's nearby dormant volcano, Mt. Edgecumbe, and the tip of Sitka National Historical Park.

Right: "Seagulls in the park" taken from Indian River bridge on a foggy morning.

Every summer in Alaska, beginning in late July, pink salmon return to the same river they hatched in. Indian River runs through Sitka National Historical Park and is home to a massive run of pink salmon. These salmon dodge eagles, seagulls and brown bears in their fight to swim upstream and lay their eggs and fertilize them in the rocky river bed. All salmon die shortly after spawning and their bodies litter the river bed.

These two photographs show salmon, both dead and alive, in Indian River. While the smell can be intoxicating at times, fall rains quickly sweep the carcasses out to the ocean where they decay and play their important roll in the ecosystem.

This totem pole also appears on the front cover of this book.

On May 15th, 2011, Sitka National Historical Park's newest totem pole named "Wooch Jin Dul Shat Kooteeya" was raised by the community. A traditional pole raising technique was used to raise this beautiful pole with manpower. This pole was designed by local Tlingit artist and carver, Tommy Joseph to mark the 100th anniversary of Sitka National Historical Park. While all totem poles are special, this pole is unique because it was designed specifically for Sitka National Historical Park and represents several different tribes on one pole, while most poles are about one specific tribe.

To raise this pole there were hundreds of people (including Grace) who held long ropes attached to the center of the pole. With direction, the community pulled this amazing totem pole into place so that it could look over our town and beautiful Mt. Edgecumbe for generations to come.

# About the Authors

Born and raised in Sitka, Alaska, Tracie Harang grew up boating and camping with her family in Southeast Alaska. Now married with three children, she loves exploring the vast, wild waterways and forests surrounding her. With a determined, adventuresome spirit, she finds her enthusiasm for the outdoors is contagious to her children. Tracie graduated from North Idaho College in 1993 with an associate arts degree. Along with writing, Tracie weaves antler baskets and is an assistant swimming coach, as well as a competitive master swimmer herself.

Grace Harang was born in Sitka, Alaska as well. She is the youngest of three kids and never one to stay behind. She is always ready for a new adventure, no matter what the weather is doing. Grace has a love of fishing and often out-fishes her brothers. Grace also loves to hike. She hiked the Mt. Edgecumbe volcano near Sitka when she was only eight years old! Grace is a competitive swimmer on the Baranof Barracuda Swim Club and was in the 4th grade in 2013.